Why Are People Different?

A Book About Prejudice

By Barbara Shook Hazen
Illustrated by Kathy Wilburn

Prepared with the cooperation of Bernice Berk, Ph.D.,
of the Bank Street College of Education

A GOLDEN BOOK • NEW YORK
Western Publishing Company, Inc.   Racine, Wisconsin 53404

Note to Parents

People are sometimes frightened by things that are different or unfamiliar. That fear can lead to hatred or prejudice. One of the most destructive things about prejudice is that it hurts everyone. The victims of prejudice are hurt, but those who perpetuate prejudice are hurt as well. That is why parents must teach their children to accept other people and their differences. Differences in people's skin color, hair color, language, dress, or religion need not be frightening. Reading WHY ARE PEOPLE DIFFERENT? together with your child can help teach this fact.

Not only must children get to know people who are different, and have ongoing relationships with them, they should also learn to be comfortable with and value people as human beings. That's what helps children value themselves as human beings as well.

—The Editors

One day after school, Terry stomped in the door, threw his guitar case on the floor, and said, "Nobody likes me because I'm different!"

"I like you," said Terry's grandma, giving him a warm, welcome-home hug.

"That doesn't count," said Terry. "You're my grandma. I hate my new school, and I hate being black. Why do I have to be different?"

"Everyone is different, one way or another," said Grandma. "I like you *because* you're different—because different is special."

"Not to me," said Terry. "Different is a drag. Different is not having anyone to sit with at lunch.

"And not being asked over after school.

"And having everyone make fun of me, like that dumb Peter who said, 'I thought all black kids were good at basketball,' today."

Grandma put her arm around Terry. "Just think what it would be like," she said, "if you went to the candy store and all the candies were exactly alike, instead of different kinds and shapes and flavors. You wouldn't like that, would you?"

Terry said, "Grandma, I'm not talking about candy. I'm talking about *me,* about feeling like I don't count."

"Well then," said Terry's grandmother, "let's talk about you. What do you do when you feel like you don't count?"

"Sometimes I try to *make* the other kids notice me," said Terry. "And sometimes I get mad.

"And other times I try to act cool, like *I* don't care.
"Once I hid under the bleachers, where no one could
see me, and cried."

"Goodness gracious," said Terry's grandma. "You do take after me. I used to do all those things when I was your age. I felt like I was the only one in the whole, wide world who was different."

"You did?" said Terry. "But back then, everyone in your school was black."

"Just because people are the same color doesn't make them the same, inside or outside," said Terry's grandma. "When I was your age, I felt different outside because I was so tall. And I felt different inside, too, because I liked climbing trees better than playing with dolls."

"What did you do?" Terry asked.

"The same sorts of things you do," said Terry's grandma.
"Sometimes I'd try to make the other girls notice me.
Other times, when they called me Beanpole or Tomboy,
I'd call them names back.

"Or I'd act like I couldn't care less. And sometimes, I'd cry."

"Then what happened?" said Terry.

"After a while, I got tired of feeling left out and upset all the time, so I decided to try to get to know some of those girls. Some of them were pretty nice. And all of them were different, one way or another."

"One girl, named Leslie, liked to climb trees, too. And another, named Elza, made me realize dolls aren't all sissy stuff."

"Pretty soon, I didn't mind being different, because I began to feel better about being me," Terry's grandmother said gently.

Then she laughed, "And I learned that being tall is sometimes an advantage, just as all kinds of differences are."

"I still feel different," said Terry. "And I still mind."

"Well, let's talk about your friends at the old school while you help me make some cookies," said Terry's grandmother, walking toward the kitchen.

"All your old friends were pretty different from each other—and from you," Terry's grandmother said as she stirred. "Lenny had a limp, Carlo had an accent, Marta wore thick glasses, and Richie was very short."

"Yeah, but I *knew* them," said Terry.

"That's just it," said Terry's grandmother, giving him a
taste. "It's getting to know people that makes you feel
more comfortable around them. Sometimes people are
afraid of things they don't understand, or someone new.
Being different shouldn't make any difference. Things will
probably get better when you and the new kids get to
know each other better."

"It isn't that simple," Terry grumbled.

"Maybe," said his grandmother. "But maybe if you
worried less about being liked, it might be easier to start
liking first."

The next day, nothing much changed at school.
But Terry kept thinking about what his grandmother said.
He began looking, really looking, at the kids in his new
school. They were all pretty different from each other,
one way or another.
Then he thought, "I wonder what that dumb kid Peter
would feel like if he was the new kid at my old school."

At lunchtime Terry leaned his guitar case against the chair and tried to look as if he didn't mind eating alone.

"Hey," came a voice. "Is that your guitar?" It was that kid Peter. He was heading straight for Terry.

"Yeah," said Terry. "What's it to you?"

"N-n-n-nothing. What I mean is, I just thought you might want to j-j-j-join our group."

Then Peter sat down next to Terry. "S-s-s-s-ometimes, what I say doesn't come out right."

"That's okay," Terry said. Then he asked, "You play guitar?"

"B-b-b-anjo," said Peter.

"Maybe we can play together sometime," said Terry.

"That's what I was thinking," said Peter with a grin.

Peter and Terry talked right through lunch. During play period, Terry met the rest of the group.

Peter didn't stutter at all when he played ball, or talked to the kids he knew. And by the time the day was over, he didn't stutter talking to Terry, either.

So when Terry asked, "How about all of you coming over after school?" Peter said, "Sure," loud and clear.

That afternoon Terry stomped into the house with his friend Peter. Nat, who played the bongos, and Chan, who had a horn, and Carla, who played the flute, were right behind him.

"Hi, Grandma," Terry called as they raced upstairs to his room. "I brought some friends with me—Peter, the kid I told you about, and a couple of others. We're going to play. Okay?"

After a few minutes Grandma put some cookies on a plate and followed the kids upstairs. Terry asked her to sit down and listen.

"Hey, that sounds good," said Peter, when they stopped for a cookie break. "I think we'll be great together."

"I think so too," said Terry. Then he smiled at Grandma, as if to say, "You're right. Being different doesn't have to make a difference. It's really getting to know someone that counts."